Notes to Parents and Teachers:

As a child becomes more familiar reading books, it is important for him/her to rely on and use reading strategies more independently to help figure out words they do not know.

REMEMBER: PRAISE IS A GREAT MOTIVATOR!

Here are some praise points for beginning readers:

• I saw you get your mouth ready to say the first letter of that word.

• I like the way you used the picture to help you figure out that word.

• I noticed that you saw some sight words you knew how to read!

Book Ends for the Reader!

Here are some reminders before reading the text:

• Point to each word you read to make it match what you say.

• Use the picture for help.

• Look at and say the first letter sound of the word.

• Look for sight words that you know how to read in the story.

• Think about the story to see what word might make sense.

Words to Know Before You Read

deaf

friend

helper

language

learn

playground

sign

special

Katie Can
KATIE MEETS CARL

By Erin Savory
Illustrated by
Marcin Piwowarski

Rourke Educational Media

A Division of
Carson Dellosa Education

Katie is
at school.

4

"This is Carl. He is new to our class."

Carl is Deaf. This means he cannot hear.

Carl has a special helper.
His helper listens
to the teacher.

He uses his hands to repeat her words for Carl. This is called sign language.

Carl's helper shows the class how to sign "hello."

Katie has never met someone who is Deaf before.

But Katie can make a new friend!

Katie has Down syndrome. She had a hard time talking when she was small.

12

So, Katie learned some sign language.
Now she wants to learn more.

"Hello! My name is Katie." Katie says.

Carl smiles and signs. "He says it is good to meet you!"

Katie shows Carl
the playground.
He runs fast!

Carl shows Katie
new words.

SLIDE

17

Carl shows Katie a photo of his dog.
Katie shows her dog too!

The class goes to the library. Katie checks out a book to learn more signs.

School is over. Katie signs "goodbye" to Carl.

Katie is happy to have
a new friend!

Book Ends for the Reader

I know...

1. What does the word deaf mean?

2. What is sign language?

3. What word does Carl teach Katie?

I think...

1. What makes a good friend?

2. Can you be friends with someone who is different from you?

3. How would you treat a new person in your class?

Book Ends for the Reader

What happened in this book?

Look at each picture and talk about what happened in the story.

About the Author

Erin Savory is a writer who lives in Florida. She has a younger sister with Down syndrome. Her sister learned some words in sign language before she could speak.

About the Illustrator

Marcin Piwowarski is an illustrator from Poland. He finds inspiration in nature and music. Marcin has worked on numerous books, including *Who is Ana Dalt?*, *You Belong*, *The Mouse in the Hammock*, and *Dibs*. He hopes his work will allow children and adults alike to explore fascinating and familiar worlds.

Library of Congress PCN Data

Katie Meets Carl / Erin Savory
(Katie Can)
ISBN 978-1-73164-900-3 (hard cover)(alk. paper)
ISBN 978-1-73164-848-8 (soft cover)
ISBN 978-1-73164-952-2 (E-book)
ISBN 978-1-73165-004-7 (e-Pub)
Library of Congress Control Number: 2021935448

Rourke Educational Media
Printed in the United States of America
01-1872111937

www.rourkeeducationalmedia.com

Edited by: Hailey Scragg
Layout by: Janeen Ruggiero
Cover and interior illustrations by: Marcin Piwowarski